To my mother, Nomsa, you make me possible. I love you.

Thank you to my father and my siblings.

Love and gratitude to my wonderful friends for their support and their guidance.

– L.M

To my daughter, Zamankwali, you are my light.

– M.M

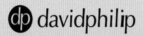

© David Philip Publishers 2018
© Text 2018 Lebohang Masango
© Illustrations 2018 Masego Morulane

Second Edition Fourth Impression
Published in 2020 by David Philip Publishers trading as New Africa Books
Unit 13, Athlone Industrial Park, 10 Mymoena Crescent, Newfields, Cape Town, 7764
www.newafricabooks.com

First published 2017 by Thank You Books

ISBN: 978-1-4856-2670-1
E pub ISBN: 978-1-4856-2710-4
E mobi ISBN: 978-1-4856-2711-1

Typesetting: Masego Morulane & Hybrid Creative

Printed and bound in the Republic of South Africa.
We are committed to a sustainable future for our business, our readers and our planet.

Mpumi's magic beads

Lebohang Masango & Masego Morulane

In Joburg city, all dull and grey,

three friends are bored at school.

It's break time and they would like to play

but there's no grass, no field or pool.

Their classes are in a big, concrete building

with offices above and shops below,

on a busy street full of people and cars

so they have no other place to go.

Mpumi sighs and twirls her black braids.

Tshiamo says: "Those beads look so pretty".

"Thank you," she replies and spins around,

"I was plaited by Tshego, my favourite aunty!"

They admire each other's beautiful hair;

Tshiamo's afro and Asante's plaits are lovely.

They smile some more but remember that they're bored.

"I wish we could have fun!" exclaims Mpumi.

The beads jingle
and jangle and sparkle.
The girls all giggle with glee.
The next thing you know,
they zoom into the air
and fly up into the clouds,
up above the city!

They land on the ground, all in a big heap;

they stand up and dust themselves slowly.

"What is this strange place we've never been?"

But it isn't the three of them only.

They see boys and girls and mamas and papas

and a whole lot of wild animals too:

a monkey, a lion, a bear, and a parrot that shouts,

"Welcome to the Johannesburg Zoo!"

The friends just can't believe it;

what an amazing, awesome surprise!

They explore the zoo; count their favourite animals

and run around with the biggest of smiles.

"How did it happen?" asks Tshiamo.

Asante really has no idea.

"Aunty Tshego says my hair is special," Mpumi offers,

"So maybe that's what brought us here."

Asante rubs her chin and thinks,

"There's only one good way to find out.

Ever seen the moon and stars up close?" she winks.

"I wish us into outer space," Mpumi shouts!

The beads jingle and jangle and sparkle.

The girls all giggle with glee.

The next thing you know, they zoom into the air

and fly up into the clouds, up above the city.

The planetarium is very dark.

The girls' eyes are as big as plates!

Above, a black sky twinkles with many, many stars.

From their seats, they stare deep into space.

There's the solar system," Tshiamo whispers,

"The planets go around the sun."

"And the one we live on is called Earth," adds Mpumi,

"It's full of life: A home for everyone."

Tshiamo says, "I'm ready for our next trip,"
Asante smiles a big smile and agrees.
"We've never been to Gold Reef City," says Mpumi.
"I wish us onto a rollercoaster," she screams.

The beads jingle and jangle and sparkle.
The girls all giggle with glee.
The next thing you know, they zoom into the air
and fly up into the clouds, up above the city.

In little red cars, safely buckled in,

the girls hold tight to the rollercoaster ride.

They laugh and scream: "Oh, we feel so dizzy!"

As they whizz and whoosh, dip and dive.

From the fantastic view, they can see their school,

Mpumi yells: "We're almost out of time!"

The rollercoaster makes its final swoop

as the girls' hearts beat faster than ever!

Eventually, it comes to a slow, slow stop

and they hop off the ride together.

"Gold Reef City is fun," pants Asante,

"But I don't want to get into trouble – let's leave!"

They get ready to go but then they hear a girl shout:

"Mommy, her hair looks like worms covered in beads!"

With tears in her eyes, Mpumi asks her friends:

"Why would someone say something so mean?"

Asante and Tshiamo feel sad now too

Because of how unhappy their best friend feels.

"I wish we could all go back," Mpumi whispers.

She really is too upset to speak.

But the beads don't jingle or jangle or sparkle

Because Mpumi is as sad as can be.

Nothing happens and the girls stand still.

Asante and Tshiamo look very worried.

But the next thing you know, they zoom into the air

And they get stuck up in the clouds, up above the city!

Oh no! The friends are stuck on Hillbrow Tower,

The tallest building in the city by far.

They look down and all that their eyes can see

Are tiny people and tiny moving dots of cars.

"This is not school. Where are we?" Asante panics.

All three friends are scared with worry.

"Oh no, the magic beads didn't work," cries Mpumi

"This is my fault. I'm so sorry!"

Mpumi sits down, covers her face and cries.

She blames herself for getting them stuck.

Tshiamo and Asante rush to give her a big hug.

"Mpumi, don't be sad. You've got us!"

Tshiamo says, "Don't let anyone get you down, Mpumi."

"You're beautiful and so are your braids."

The girls pull faces and make jokes.

All to get Mpumi smiling once again.

In no time, it works as her face lights up.

See? Nothing is too difficult when you have friends!

The girls all feel good and glad now,

they stand up and get ready to go.

Feeling full of love and holding hands,

"I wish us back to school!"

"I wish us back to school!"

"I wish us back to school!" their voices echo.

The beads jingle and jangle and sparkle.

The girls all giggle with glee.

The next thing you know, they zoom into the air

and fly up into the clouds, up above the city.

The girls are safe, back at school and happy,

They had such a fun time exploring.

Mpumi, Tshiamo and Asante are the best of friends

And now they know: Joburg city is not at all boring.